# Become Traditionally Published

in today's wild and woolly literary media climate

H.L. Dowless

# Contents

## The Odyssey Begins

Hello, I am author, H.L. Dowless. While I have worn many hats in my life, the one I have worn with a continuing consistency is that of writer, designer, and creator. I have been traditionally published by hundreds of literary journals, magazines, anthologies, zines, e-zines, and numerous publishing companies. Having such success is the supreme goal of nearly every person who enjoys writing. In all honesty, accomplishing this desired goal in today's writing and publishing climate can seem daunting, and frustrating, to say the least. *However, what separates contracts from incessant lines of rejection notes, is a step by step plan of action.*

In fact, what you are observing before you is a piece of how-to information tough to acquire, I am sad to say, even in today's information age. What I am speaking of when I say the word, *information,* are specifically detailed techniques bearing constant results, with a noticeable potential for dramatic increase. I know well what every beginning writer is up against, and more often than not, even seasoned writers. From these experiences emerged this proven strategy, and if steps are followed in exact detail, can potentially deliver practitioners a dramatic increase in traditional publishing success!

While I could bore you with details regarding my own personal writing life philosophy and my own daily living notes as a person, an author, and writer, it is much more my nature as an individual person to dim the lamp light, and get down to the bone of what this subject matter is all about. What this lesson is about is *how a person can start from scratch as a rookie writer with a high level of interest and motivation, hone his craft, and break into the market at a bottom level;  set his sights on higher goals, court a following in his art, and consequently achieve traditional publishing success, in continuum.*

# The Situation

The world of writing, authorship, and publishing today is in a pickle. Its not the first time in history where such a situation has been prevalent, but so it is with the time era we presently live in. In the beginning, writing was done by scribes from wealthier classes educated in the craft. Publishing co-ops (*companies if you will*), hired a dozen or more scribes to hand write and copy a single manuscript multiple times. Scrolls and manuscripts were produced utilizing expensive materials, and the general audience was limited to the well educated, often living in the monasteries or in university extensions thereof. Thus the produced works were limited to the wealthier audience therein, catering to their specific cultural and educational concerns. A need for writers and their works was greatly limited as a result. A vast majority of talented, potentially interested people, were locked out of the broad system in consequence, if they could become educated to write at all.

Outside the monasteries were the traveling troubadours and minstrels, but these people functioned solely in the many taverns and festival street shows,  only utilizing the spoken word to repeat long held oral traditions, facilitating an audience with its own concerns for entertainment and information, who was largely far less privileged and totally illiterate. The new technologies changing all of this forever were the *press and the printing press machine.*

The first presses were blocks of wood with 3D letters carved on them. Individual pages of manuscripts were carved onto a single wooden block or board in 3D, then manually hand stamped onto sheets of quasi-inexpensive papyrus paper rather than vellum. Now manuscripts could be produced in much larger volume, lowering the prices of books and written material in general. More people were now motivated to become educated, outside of a single specific socioeconomic class line. Thus there was a greater need for skilled writers, their works, literacy instructors,  and hand-press operators.

Certain nameless writers then became well known during their own lifetimes, beyond a specific locality, maybe for the first time in history. An embrace of the broad proletariat masses, however, was still yet to come.

Time passed, and these blocks and boards were mounted onto pedal operated wooden machines, where a seated operator pushed pedals with his feet, motivating the board, block, and later metal stamps to print entire manuscript sheets. This new technology greatly reduced the time frame for printing manuscripts. The end result was that books, news letters, and pamphlets, fell far more in price.

Far more people could now access this information. Isolated communities learned of presently occurring world wide events, and the publishing world needed far more writers, journalists, and writing creatives in general. An era of time eventually emerged when people who wrote could actually consider writing as a respectable living standard sustaining craft, or a skilled trade if you will, where need was greater than the supply of those capable in performing the writing services or operating the printing mechanism. Many more once nameless writers, or those only famous locally, now became famous nationally, or internationally in the passage of time.

Time passed again, and the next improvement of technology built upon that which stood before it. This great event occurred when the printing press moved from being peddle operated, to steam engine operated. Maybe no other event of history, other than the press itself, even came close to expanding public access to printed material of all types. Now people needed to be able to read, as the system at large increasingly operated based on the written word. More people became literate and far better educated, as a result. The need for writers, teachers of writing discipline, their works, and creatives at large, far exceeded the supply. The realm of locally known or nameless writers, expanded to allow those among them to reach fame and fortune nationally and internationally, greater than ever before. There were chronic time chunks where the economy slumped, need subsided, and fame or fortune was lost, but these situations *always* arrived and passed.

The point in this talk of writing history is that *we,* of our own era, *are in one of those times where the field has been saturated with creative works, and those who are producing them.* Because of computer technology, authors, individually owned publishers, and printers, have many more choices besides the traditional route. The self-publishing route is vastly becoming more viable and competitive, as the traditional route becomes increasingly saturated. Nowadays mid-level and top publishers want artists who can deliver selling products, and nothing less. The most basic bottom level publishers are becoming more discerning in what they choose to accept. Very soon paying to have ones work published may not be enough to enter inside this ever saturating market. Cost free avenues are already discriminating based on quality considerations.

In the age prior to the computer era, publishers would often take a calculated chance on unknown rookie authors who appeared to have promise, but such reality is simply *not the case anymore* in most instances. Publishers have bills to pay, and like all businesses, absolutely must function somewhere above the break even margin; or else they shut their doors and simply fade away. This understanding explains why one's top surface publisher choices are more narrow now than in the past hundred plus years. Mid and bottom level publishers often twinkle like stars turning on and burning out, in a dreary intimidating night-time panorama.

Rather than simply give in to the self publishing option, which is very difficult to become successful doing, since most self published books only sell around two hundred copies; *one needs to focus his best efforts toward becoming traditionally published.* When at least seventy five failed submissions have been made, with accompanying periodic editorial and interior manuscript changes made along the way, the self publishing options are fine to engage. *The first seventy five submissions, however, should be directed toward traditional options.* While attempting such a feat can become very discouraging, even to a seasoned author, the difference between success and failure, *is a defined strategy for success.*

Behold, dear observer, this direct very effective strategy is what you are on the cusp of receiving, in all of its most simplified glory.

## The Strategy

Imagine today's publishing realm as a huge media ocean. Traditional publishers, like most in this vast primeval, whale eat shark sea, may be divided into three classes. We have bottom feeders, which discriminate mind you, but only at a bottom level. We have mid-level publishers, which is where a majority of our independent and even university publishers fall. Then we have our leviathan surface feeders, who are absolute gluttons for the best feeding material available in this vast informational sea. These top feeders are also those who form the *supreme apex* of our writer's submission efforts.

As one may have already ascertained, these top feeders are most difficult for *rookie writers and a majority of other skill levels,* to land a contract with; short of some best selling author on the self publishing circuit, an extremely rare breed indeed! My absolute favorite example lies in the kind lady, *Amanda Hockings*. When in need of some exemplary fact based reading material, click up details of this lady's life.

What I am proposing in this informational body is a plan for building one's writing crafts and products up in the public mind, as the effort to becoming traditionally published is being simultaneously made. Unfortunately, this sometimes means including details of our personal lives in with this constructive effort. Those who know our works, often love knowing dirty intimate details about us poor struggling authors and artists. *This is called building an author's platform.*

One will soon learn exactly how this author built a reading platform of over one hundred thousand readers inside a six month period of time. Contrary to what others may claim, having a platform is a prerequisite, when one makes his appeal to the sweet queens seated on the big thrones, in the grand castles high up on the publishing hill. Among these gorgeous dollies are where publishing contracts netting bragging rights in fifty thousand dollar advances, can still yet be secured. While having blood

or relationship connections could vastly improve one's chances of landing a contract with the big boys,

this work is intended for those who don't, yet *know they have excellent product,* while relying only on

their own efforts, starting from absolutely nothing in knowledge or resources.

In an all encompassing summary, our strategy is to commence our efforts by making first appeal to

the bottom feeders in this vast media ocean. Having some kind of success when we make our appeal, is

far better than having none at all, no matter how excellent our work is. Once we have a wide range of

success on the bottom level, then we can appeal to the mid-level range, contests, articles, etc. There

eventually comes a day when mid-level is no longer sufficient, following a decent number of

publishing successes; and we commence our appeal to literary agents, and those massive but oh so

beautiful Orca whales swimming at the surface level.


## The Cherished Techniques


Now we are at the part where everybody wants to be. These are the proven how-to tricks nobody else

is speaking to the others about. Maybe my work will change some of that, if the new information can

net positive results. Once the day arrives where I finally achieve best seller status (*30k + single book

purchases),* be rested assured, I will let consumers of my information have access to the specific how-

to skinny on the subject material.

(1) It goes without saying, *writers seeking to make any kind of submissions, absolutely must have the

highest in quality work.* I could not count the times where I submitted manuscripts that were courtly

rejected multiple times, only to delve down into it on days where my inclinations were with me, and

discover very obvious editorial mistakes that should have never been. *There must be a detailed plot that can be followed by the reader. Characters absolutely must be developed.* All of this applies even to the craziest, most creative stories told on the written page, or the most detailed and direct, nonfiction information. There absolutely *must be* an organized progression layout, or blue print, if you will.

Editors are butchers, so develop thick alligator skin, and keep on pushing your highest quality manuscripts with confidence anew. Even the best of us often have editors cruelly brutalize work we sank our creative souls into. Keep in mind, however, when editors say anything at all, it's *always* a positive sign! Observe for veiled suggestions in a feign of insult, bearing potential to improve our work, and future work efforts. People often pay hundreds for such editorial suggestions. Some writers recommend hiring one's own editor prior to making submissions to publishing companies or literary agents, but with this work partly about becoming an accomplished writer for the least financial expense possible, I would never suggest such a thing.

I could write an entire how-to volume on the subject alone, but I have my best product when I *use an outline*, especially when I write novels. I can isolate my individual characters in circles, then ask myself about his or her positive and negative personality details, looks, style of walking and speaking, or eccentric characteristics in general. I can draw lines out from these circles with one word descriptive notes on the free end. This is how I develop my characters.

I run my entire scenery through the five senses, making the same types of branches out from it, with one word notes on the free ends of the lines. When developing my plot in general, I ask the ageless six journalistic questions; *who, what, why, where, when, and how,* then thoroughly give myself written answer to these questions. The end results in making such an effort are positive for both becoming traditionally published and building one's platform, so thus, in doing so we slay two turkeys with the same sling stone.

All of this may sound time consuming and rather complicated, but after following through, when the writing actually begins, the flow is very brisk. There is no pondering or pausing! All that one must do is write, which is always good for us, because writing is what writers are best at.

(2) *Develop a personalized system for writing and making submissions.* I write at least one page or poem a day. When the feeling motivates, I do more. My typed pages allow five hundred words, single spaced, thus one might say I do no less than five hundred words a day, every day. Not only will this allow one to develop his craft, it will also allow himself to keep at least one hundred submissions out at all times. Aiming toward this specific number may sound crazy, but no matter how extraordinary one's plot is, how elegant the word flow, or how skillful the editorial efforts made; truth is, *if writing is not submitted, it will never become published!* Write the work, allow it to sit for thirty days, carefully edit it out three times, allowing it to sit for another month between each edit, then submit it. Keep a backlog of submit-able work always on hand.

(a) When one begins making submissions, utilize a free *submissions platform.* There are outstanding one's that charge fees, such as *Duotrope,* but my information is for writers who are cost conscious, and may not have access to extra financial resources. That being said, Duotrope does have a free version, and may be worth while to investigate.

Any methodology effective writer's utilize is better than simply googling for poetry, short story, article, or novel submission channels. Virtually every avenue listed on google is saturated by submissions, or is filled with the lowest forms of predatory feeders in our hypothetical media ocean, the *vanity press.* It goes without saying, but we should always seek to avoid any type of predator.

This ultra-poisonous cuttlefish in our media ocean often attempts to hide behind a veil of legitimacy by labeling itself as a *hybrid publisher,* listing itself throughout the googled realm. That being said, there are hybrid publishers who might be worth one's while to carefully examine, if one's desire lies in such a direction. In many instances, the web-listing and its accompanying dangerous site, is near impossible for writers to identify. By utilizing a submissions platform, we effectively bypass these creatures seeking to do us, our finances, and our precious creative efforts harm. When any slight possibility for danger exists, our handy dandy submissions platform tells us so, in clear precise and specific details.

We may make personalized selection requests, such as eliminating journals who charge for submissions, and directing our submissions toward those who only accept mailed in manuscripts. We may also choose from those who are accepting poetry, short stories, articles, novels, novellas, and novelettes. Our submission engine will also inform me if I have submitted to a particular company in the past.

Never submit again before the first submission has been examined. At times its polite and in professional form to ask the editor if one may make another submission. While I have mailed manuscripts in, I virtually *always choose to email my submissions*. Not only is doing so far less expensive and cumbersome, it allows me to utilize a systemic approach to the question of making effective submissions.

My personal approach to submitting is to make three individual company submissions a day, and no less. These submissions can constitute more than one piece to three different companies. It is best, however, to only make a single submission per company, I feel, except when the company clearly states that doing otherwise is acceptable. Read the submission guidelines well to determine of one's story is right for the company in question.

Distinguishing the lowest, but safe, bottom feeders in our media sea is really simple. Giving specific working examples may prove to be counter productive here, but one now defunct example I used in my early days, was *American Star Publishing*. I actually had acceptable results in spite of the negative remarks regarding this company. These relatively safe bottom feeders are those companies who publish huge numbers of works, and generally offer only mediocre editorial efforts at best. These companies *do not*, however, *publish any and every piece submitted*. Not even ASP did this, no matter what its disgruntled authors and critics might claim.

After seventy five failed submissions to companies of higher standing in this bottom category, we may choose to submit our own well edited manuscripts to these bottom level companies accepting nearly anything, for marketing purposes alone. I prefer those offering print and e-book versions of my work. If one really finds himself in a rejection pickle, another good possibility is *Free e-books.net*.

Here one will not get paid, but can have a professionally designed cover for free, and more than likely receive a massive number of downloads; there again, spreading his author name, his work, and building his publishing platform. If one possesses a professionally designed cover and wants to net a paycheck, other great possibilities when in a rejection pickle are *Smashwords* and *Draft to Digital*, both of whom I have used. If one seeks to secure his fortune with these companies, however, never bet your head on it.

These platforms at the lowest level in our vast media sea will allow us to harvest readers in tens of thousands, who may readily examine us as skilled authors and our work for content and quality. Keep in mind as well, that often big name publishing companies, the beautiful Orcas in our hypothetical media sea, will cruise passed these hideaway realms, seeking new creative morsels for consumption. Nameless writers have gained valuable recognition here and launched successful writing careers, although realistically the odds are highly against such occurrences, so please don't bet your writing life on it ever happening. Great marketing boosts for one's material are always available for a nominal fee, on most of these sites.

More than likely in these places, we will always succeed in getting our work accepted for publication. Having our author's name and work out via some sort of avenue, is better by far, than not having it out at all. Otherwise there are only four remaining options worth mentioning here for us to use.

(b) *The submission grinder.*   This avenue is the basic work horse of my personal submission efforts, in all forms. TSG is the/a totally free version of Duotrope. Maybe 90% of publishing entities listed fall into the mid-level range. I recommend prospective authors to eventually focus one's primary submission efforts toward this category, which is highly discriminating. While I choose those companies who publish more than thirty works a year, giving my work a greater chance, often these companies only publish 10 manuscripts, or even fewer. Many companies and journals listed, have thousands of subscribers, if I understand the notes on their websites right; meaning that upon publication of my works, I have the same number of readers. Even if these companies do not offer pay, one is still building up his platform among the masses. It is very possible that in the future these mid level publishers may also gain high ranking in respectability inside the vast media sea and literary world, making them and their offerings highly sought after. When we obtain publishing success herein, our names and works are consequently recognized, right along with the company at large.

(c) *Submittable* -  As one makes his submissions, many literary journals, magazines, and publishing companies use Submittable to manage their submissions. While Submittable is not the only one, it is certainly the most commonly encountered submissions manager. One may also utilize the same manager to discover new avenues for making submissions.

Simply click *"discover"* at the top of the site. When the site search bar appears, click in it and seek out whatever category one is trying to submit unto, be it novel, short story, etc. Click on this. Click the free button for companies who don't charge submission fees, and soon one will have his selection of choices. When I use up all of my potential choices in TSG, often I go here. There are also listings for contests, universities seeking new writers work, author residencies for one to apply to, etc. It will not harm anything to simply browse through here on occasion, as the feeling to do so leads.

(d) *Author's Published Magazine*- If I recall right, I think I actually paid a one time fee of $12.00 American, for access to this delightful online magazine, but the minimal fee was well worth it, I feel. What I get is a thoroughly researched list of mid-level publishing companies and other information valuable to authors, that virtually always fulfills two in my daily submission goal of three. On more than a few occasions I can book a complete three for the entire week, out of this avenue alone, and never have a worry about any form of predator lurking about in our vast media sea!

(e) *Freedom With Writing* – Although some of these listings can be of questionable character, meaning *higher quality hybrid publishers*, most to be found are worth the effort of writers making submissions to. For the reason noted above, I almost neglected mentioning this listing of publishers, but then again, this listing is an avenue I have used in the past and had traditional success with, though not much. This site lists contests, newly emerging journals and very small publishing companies. Readers will have to be their own judge in regard to efforts spent searching here being worthwhile. Drop a note and let me know about your personal experiences.

(f) Other neat places to find journals and publishers where one may submit work are *Creative Writers Opportunity List, Entrophy, Poets & Writers, & New Pages.* Between these sources prospective writers should never exhaust their options.

Before we move on there is one final note. Expect rejections! Before my first traditional publishing success I had a short story laying on hand for twenty years. The title was *"King Of Cat."* According to my notes I had fifty rejections before I ever had one single acceptance, of any story or writing at all. Short stories seem to be the easiest to have published. Articles are next. Poems fall somewhere into third place. Novellas and novelettes come next in place. Last in place are novel submissions.

Out of all writing efforts, I have found that having my novels accepted is toughest for me to pull off. For that reason, when I submit my novel manuscripts, I make three additional daily submissions to individual publishing companies in that category alone. One is also free to be creative in his own approach to fulfilling the objective.

In summary, dutifully follow the prescribed format. No matter how many rejections arise, keep editing, revising, and submitting. Do this because one loves creating, writing, and seeing one's work in print, be it online or in hand. Take great pride in knowing that being accepted by a third party via scrutiny by this third party, says far more for one's literary artistry than merely paying a company to publish it or simply uploading a PDF into some online site. Vow to keep up the daily rhythm until health deterioration or one's death prevents it.

I can honestly promise here that *one's writing success is virtually guaranteed* in the energy spent, on one level or another. I have found that virtually every aspiration in life follows the identical formula, with the same guarantee for success, if only we pledge to *cease not* in our attempts. In the end, while we may not be Dickens, Hemingway, or Stephan King, but by God, we still got our feet inside the golden doorway of possibility. Like winning the lottery, the only way to literally guarantee raffle or publishing failure, is to forbear on buying lottery tickets or making writing submissions.

## Marketing

Believe it or not, when we initiate our court with the elegant surface feeders in this vast hypothetical media sea, we are actually embracing the virtues of marketing, no matter what expert should disagree with this conclusion, nor the contesting remarks following it. Once we have attained an array of traditional publishing success with the mid-level feeders, we may then validate our position for being talented in the field, and fully qualified to make our forthcoming higher appeal. Sadly, while certainly not an absolute prerequisite; in this day and age the higher our potential sales volume, the more attractive our appeal.

Virtually all of our surface feeders demand us to reach out toward them through *agents*. Landing an agent is much more challenging than being traditionally published, I feel.  A list of active agents and their employing companies may be extrapolated and derived inside this link; https://querymanager.com/users.php .

The process for writing queries to agents, is essentially the same for writing a cover sheet when we submit novel manuscripts to mid-level publishers. Matter of fact, when my western novel, *"They Called Him Ringo Arenas,"* was finally accepted for publication, I used the same query when I made my cover letter in my submission to the publishing editor, that I used in my submission to an agent.

My publisher, in this case, was upper mid-level, since I had submitted to a large number of agents, and directly to several publishers. However, to land contracts with real bragging rights, we are called upon to focus our efforts toward landing agents, who literally form a virtual glass ceiling in our hypothetical media ocean, no matter how much we may want to tell ourselves otherwise. That being said, there well may exist valid techniques for marketing self-published works of high quality, that would consistently invite best-seller status. Clear informative how-to details on this subject will have to wait until a later publication, however.

Our query should commence with a hook. The agent's attention must be captured inside the first one or two sentences. Feed the agent only enough to pull him or her in. This is the reason I say writing query letters is a form of marketing, since we really are literally reaching out in anticipation of selling our own work.

The toughest part to master in regard to writing queries may be the body, in my opinionated opinion. Inside this body we literally have no choice but to summarize our entire novel, in maybe four or five lines. In other words, we must select a few individual words that speak virtual sentences. To get a better feel for what is being said, investigate descriptive clips on the back side of books in the local book store or library. In many instances these descriptive clips originated directly out of the query sent in to the agent, except we authors making our queries must use fewer words, in many instances!

Our conclusion is a final direct appeal where we attempt to explain how an agent or editor will benefit from having our work inside his or her publishing portfolio. Do this in a very tasteful tactful manner. We want to say what we need to, but not in an obtrusive, if not obnoxiously obvious way. In so doing we speak volumes about ourselves as creative artists and professionals. Keep in mind that the entire query should *never be over 300 words*, according to my own experience and advice from all the experts.

Sometimes agents will give very informative replies when we make our query appeal. *Always* modify the query, incorporating these suggestions, as is also true with editors. Such corrective criticism is a rare treat from people who are almost always short on time, and high on piling work. Keep making appeal after appeal, even if it takes years, and *never quit or give up. Make this and your entire writing venture your obsessive life vow*, to the point that others surrounding you may question your sanity, as I have. Do this, and I can *guarantee* you success on one level or another!

In the end I am right there in the trenches with you, slinging muddy dirt and slugging it out with our adversaries. When I finally reach best seller status, you may be rested assured that I will stand by your side and let you in on all the juicy how-to details!

Here is an example of my own query for "*They Called Him Ringo Arenas*." Feel free to adapt this letter to your own creative circumstance and situation. *Always* save copies of letters that net positive results. These can be modified to fit new novels and query situations. Carefully examine those notes failing to make the mark. Try to figure out why the query failed. If the agent or editor does not offer suggestions, then make the appropriate changes, and always resubmit elsewhere. It may take dozens of submissions before one courts attention from agents. Like horseshoes, hand grenades, and women, "*close*" counts with high marks in this game of literary submission also.

*Never* take any form of rejection personal, nor harsh repugnant remarks. Imagine yourself as being a stone statue, dedicated by future masses to your honor from your splendid past contributions to the literary world. Ask yourself would screamed rude and crude words affect a stone statue? Then turn around and resubmit elsewhere, like these negative remarks were never made.

*Dear editorial team,*

*Nothing beats a good 44000 word western, wed with a realistic plot filled by rich intrigue and exotic mystery. Top that off with a grand addition of violence in measured cups, mixed in with a light sprinkling of sexual escapade, and one might cook up a beautiful novel well worth taking a bite from. When I was composing this work, the thought struck me to go one more step farther, intending to make my unique serving irresistible; I served this dish up before a clear panorama of open, cloudless skies, cacti desert and colorful native tribes, complete with a mountainous horizon. The tin and board small towns, complete with banks, Federal Marshals, and safes filled with golden coin, really do make my special dish all that much more inviting!*

*Imagine yourself, if for only a fleeting moment, on a beach side cottage porch somewhere, immersing yourself into this exotic world of "They Called Him Ringo Arenas," I have created. Inside the American populous at large, there still lies a powerful adoration for the heritage of liberty and raw freedom my created scene represents. I anticipate a future void in the literary market of today for these types of scenes. My short readable novel is one seeking to fill that void, being relatively brisk, making it easy to read on a variety of electronic devices, or in an accompanying print form.*

*Hollywood literally built its empire from such compact novels. Who knows, mine might be the next novel to make its mark on Hollywood's list of accomplishments, with your kind assistance, of course! I am cordially inviting you to be a part of this pleasant development of mine. Please let me know if you are interested. I anxiously await your answer.*

*Sincerely*

*H.L. Dowless*

According to more than six experts in the publishing field I interviewed at a literary convention once upon a time, there are a set of consistent specific reasons why queries fail. These reasons are:

(1) Poor formatting- looks like a craft project with text. No personality

(2) Not to the point with the information. It comes in an attachment, so its not personal, a huge DON'T!

(3)  It exceeds the unspoken 300 word limit.

(4) Fails to relate the book toward the agent's expectations or answer the question of why the work is worth the agent or editor's time.

(5) The author attempted to pitch more than one manuscript inside the same query, a great big DON'T.

(6) Pitched prior to finishing the manuscript, although doing so with non-fiction is alright.

(7) Did not follow the agent's rules listed inside the submission requirements.

(8) Queried the wrong agent for the genre'- an easy mistake that I have made numerous times.

(9) Best advice- harvest the names of at least 50 agents in one's genre' before submitting once.

As should already be apparent, good marketers would instinctively know to do these things when writing queries. Maybe one could hire a marketer to write these special notes of appeal, although I have never done such a thing. Having a family member, close friend or associate, who is a professional marketeer, should help tremendously.

Here is another example of an effective query garnished from the advice of these experts at the literary convention I once attended. By the way, one's attendance at literary conventions is an extraordinarily effective method for us nameless authors, to secure relationships with agents and editors employed by those gorgeous Orca surface feeding queens in our hypothetical media ocean. Take your pick, my example or theirs.

Dear ( *agent's name*), I noticed that you represent (*name of an author they represent*). I loved ( *agent's recent books*) and because I write ( *genre*) too, I feel like you would be perfect to represent my novel (*novel title*). I have been submitting my novels only to bottom level independent publishers up until this point because (*reason here if true. Your publishing achievement, for example,*) *My last novel i.e. publication successes hit number* ___ *in the sales charts and why it's relevant. I have a following of* (___ *number here*) through social media, online marketing sites, and my email list. The novel I'd love to have you represent is ( *pitch* ). I feel like it would slot nicely into the market alongside works such as ( *comparable titles here*). If you would like to know more, or have any question, please contact me anytime via email (*your email address here*) or telephone (*your telephone number*). Regards, (*your name*)

Below is an actual working model based on the instructions above. Notice how specifics particular to one's book in question fit in. This is only a single example from a virtual multitude of possibilities. To be frank, this example based directly on the model above, didn't work for me! Bearing the specifics and prior advice in mind, I had to take an alternative approach, which is offered above.

Dear Mrs. Little Annie Dough Jo, I noticed that you represent E. Hemingway. I loved For "*Whom The Bell Tolls*,"  and because I write adventure thrillers too, I feel you would be perfect to represent my novel "They Called Him Ringo Arenas." I have submitted my novels, novelette, novellas, short stories, and poems to many publishers of varying rank, seeking to gain experience in the publishing and marketing industry. All of my work, other than my novels, reached fairly high ranking on Amazon in both the US UK, and EU at large, and I feel my strengths lie in quality of my craft, broad appeal, and use of online social networking. I have a following of over 20K people through my booksie account, my magazine & literary journal publications, and my ultra informative writer's blog. Should you desire to know more, then contact me by phone (number) or e-mail (here).

While we are submitting our manuscripts to agents, we are still under obligation to market our prior accepted work with the mid-level and bottom feeders. That's right, in our present publishing era, we authors must engage in our own marketing efforts. Always keep in mind that in so doing, we build up our own author platform by making our work easily accessible to our reading audience. Our sole motivation should never be about securing our fortune, but about making ourselves known to the public. In so doing, our sought after fortune may well come with this personal effort spent on our part.

(1) *Carefully analyze the entities whom one submits to.* Choose print journals and magazines with anthologies, where the subscription audience is at least 100k, or close to it. If one has been through a continuing succession of submission failures, then any number will work, to be honest. Online entities with more than a hundred thousand viewers or subscribers, would work out O.K. Yet in the end, anything is better than nothing. Our goals should *always be high,* within reason at the onset, however, since our quality product demands it.

Once upon a time I discovered a publisher who operated from a literary dispensary system found throughout a well respected university campus and town. This publisher agreed to process several of my poems and flash fiction pieces of 1000 words or less. Their acceptance of my work was a great marketing score, I feel. Not only are college students and professors avid readers, generally speaking, often many university administrative officials hold solid contacts inside the publishing establishment.

All it takes is one qualified suggestion from a single well connected individual, to make a difference between recognized success, and enduring anonymity.

At any rate, at least one's name and work will be seeded out to potentially thousands of readers, in an environment where the written word endures for the long term. Seeding out forms the basic philosophy for my personal marketing effort. One day in the future there may well be a bountiful harvest made for the effort spent, since we *always* reap what we sow, eh?

(2) *Open a booksie account online.* Here one may seed out samples of his work. I tend to do this with pieces that I absolutely cannot find a publisher for. In the days prior to computer technology, these works would have been trashed, or merely cast aside in an attic shoe-box somewhere. I first do a careful edit and often rewrite these.  On this site one may communicate with his audience, commend, receive comments, open his own publishing company!, etc. In a six month period of time I raised more than 50k readers, and many dozens of subscribers on this site. There are always contests and chances to market to a huge audience available for a small fee on a booksie site. Take full advantage of everything this opportunity has to offer.

(3) *Start one's own author blog.* This method is a genuine no-brainier. There is an honest tact and technique to the effort, however. Make one's blog entirely dedicated to one's author life and his writing. An entirely different blog may be utilized for other concerns. My own author blog can be found at Rowdy Living Press .

A reading audience loves knowing about intimate details in an author's personal life, so long as it relates to his work. Speak freely about one's personal adventures, while relating it back to his writing. Maintain a travel diary, as I did when we spent more than three months in Spain recently. I said I was creating my own author's writing retreat, which in fact I was! I told readers specifically how I went about this, as I informed them of my day to day experiences.

On another page have vivid working links to ones published work, telling about that work in detail. Have no less than ten links. One's entire author page with Amazon would be extraordinarily fine to link! Here all of one's works available with Amazon would be at the reader's finger tips. All marketing efforts should *always link back up to this blog*, no matter what. The idea here is to drive potential purchasing traffic to ones blog.

If one could afford purchasing TV time, then don't forget to display a link back to the author blog. *Have a professional design the blog.* I didn't to be honest, but maybe I should have, and well may at a future time. The blog is maybe the most important aspect of one's marketing campaign today. *All reading traffic is directed back to the blog.* This fundamental marketing aspect can never be emphasized enough. Link one's blog in with his personal e-mail. E-mail is said to be an effective marketing device on its own terms. A fine example of a working author's blog may be accessed above (4) Link one's blog to a site called *Connection Builder.* Here one's site can be distributed and linked automatically with 101 sites. In my case, actual connection was made with only 25, but my blog's analytic page informed me that readership literally jumped by great leaps and bounds. For only $10.00 one may upgrade and be linked with a 1000 sites,  and more sites for more money. Do this, if finances allow.

As one makes submissions to publishers, journals, magazines, etc, when they allow a blog link to be included, never forbear on doing so. Make art and photographic submissions using one's author name. Should these be accepted, the journal's publications will still reach a large audience, and one's photographs will link back to one's author name, and one's author name back to one's written work.

(5) It goes without saying that in our day and age, any business link, including those from writer's blogs, are to be uploaded on Facebook, Twitter, Instagram, Pinterest, and practically any other form of social media avenue available.  Doing so often pays off in unexpected ways.

Not long ago I spent three months in Ecuador, South America. During this time my wife and I traveled the country giving lectures on education related topics. I wrote the presentations and assisted in facilitating the events, and my wife actually made the primary parts of our presentations. When I stepped in it was at the final conclusive phase of our lecture. In addition to tying up our presentations, I very tactfully mentioned my writing, often only handing out pamphlets with descriptions and links. I also sold individual copies of my work related to education.

When our presentations concluded and our audience rushed up to speak with us, take pictures in our company, etc, I was amazed when several in the group informed me they were already my writing fans! Many of the editions from my publications were printed in multiple languages, including Spanish. Evidently links going to these publications were harvested from Facebook and Twitter, being circulated by a multiplicity of fellow users, into possibly a vast universal realm!

In our present day one never knows who is reading or looking at what, from where, when we create and utilize available marketing avenues. Be aware this emerging reality could work well for us, or against us. *Enjoy life, but never do, write, photograph, or allow to be photographed, anything one couldn't rise up and walk away from later on. Always utilize a thoroughly calculated effective veil when a tempting* opportunity presents itself as a philosophically conflicting, if not uncomfortable circumstance or situation demanding it. If such an effective cover can't be devised, or the consequential condemnation too great to chance, then simply forbear on putting the material out to the public.

(6) *Create attractive business cards with one's author blog link by the hundreds.* One may design and purchase these right online from a variety of sites. Place these cards inside the back cover pockets of

library books, and those at bookstores on subjects one writes about. Magazines found in grocery stores work fine.

Recently we made a splendid weekend mini-vacation trip to the Noah's Ark and Creation Museum exhibit in Williamstown, Kentucky.  Since I often write about ancient civilizations and creation belief systems, this visit generated a perfect scenario for me to market my own material. I casually sauntered through the souvenir shops, tactfully dropping my elegantly crafted blog cards into purses, books, and virtually any avenue where I felt people would notice and pick it up. As a general rule, those who visited this exhibit tended to be intellectual, conservative, relatively well educated, and the types who may well be motivated into purchasing material from my blog. When marketing, one must always know who his audience is, then make a direct appeal.

Public peg boards often found in stores such as Walmart, and street side light poles found in places where people congregate are fine places to pin one's blog card.  Possibilities are endless.

## Secret Direct Marketing Techniques

These are personally developed techniques. While we appreciate an ability to generate wealth, at our initiating stage doing so *should not be* our primary goal. There lies huge potential for generating an honest fortune in our techniques, since all of these fall underneath my philosophy of us reaping in what we sow out.

Truth is, no matter what we may create or write, out of the human population at large, somewhere stands a potential audience. All that we must do to find this audience is *produce quality material*, and make it available to as many people as is possible. These secret techniques are designed to function on this premise alone.

(1) *Buy thirty or more of one's own print copies,* then donate them to every library in the area. Plan a trip through multiple counties, donating copies to every library in the county. In many places all one must do is write *donated copy* on the leaf, then drop it in the return box. Areas known in advance to be literary avenues or depots, are my favorite places to target.

University towns are great places to target. Towns where publishing companies thrive are among my favorite for depositing my work. Practically any area with a growing intellectual community would be a fine place for targeting one's book donations. I have even been known to physically place my own books into book stores, but doing so is not recommended as being a best move. The only problem with library deposits is that one's books may become swamped by so many others. In consideration of this fact, we authors may still yet need a more direct approach; but at least we will have our piece held in place and circulated one way or the other, for the long term, potentially.

(2) *Drop multiple copies of one's books,* preferably on a multiplicity of subjects, inside *Lending Tree dispensaries* found throughout America. What makes Lending Tree better than its competitors for our purpose, is where they donate to libraries nationally and internationally, places we may or may not ever get to visit. Attaching one's blog card inside a book cover before dropping it in is not a bad idea.

Google the site up for Lending Tree. A map will display on this site revealing the location with an address, of every book LT dispensary box in America. Make a mini-vacation visiting dispensaries and libraries depositing one's own material. When taking vacation wherever it may be, keep these possibilities in mind for marketing one's own written material.

(3) One of my favorite most direct techniques for literally placing my work into the hands of potential readers, is by dropping a copy of my work into the many *Little Free Libraries* in my area. LFL is the greatest growing phenomenon in promoting literacy. Having one seems to be the chick thing for communities, businesses, down town areas,  and people of substance to have. I, myself, am contemplating having one, if I might establish it at the certain place I envision having one. Having one

would be *outstanding for promoting one's own work*, if done underneath proper circumstances and presentations, I feel. Since virtually any person could own and establish a LFL in his own front yard, there is an honest technique for picking out the right ones to deposit our work into, for facilitating our own specified purposes.

Little Free Library has a map on its website. This map has an address. I prefer to select areas having lots of traffic, and intellectual traffic when I can make the selection in preference. These areas include post offices, parks- especially locally visited and appreciated ones, universities, downtown areas- especially downtown touristic areas, parks and campuses of local technical colleges, bus, subway, and train stations, etc. Sometimes parks have a LFL near the children's play ground. Children's literature might be the wisest choice herein for making a deposit and attracting an audience. However, parents and their adult friends watching the children play, may desire a more intellectually challenging or entertaining read. Taylor ones informational deposits to the situation people most often find themselves in while at the particular location in question. Keep any deposit of ones creative material in line with his potential audience contained in the area.

Never deposit any sort of morally or socially questionable material into places where its not already invited. More than likely some sort of cameras are posted nearby, or some sideline, yet attentive individual, might connect one's face with the material held into question. Then one has created a Frankenstein monster who will follow him incessantly, maybe even to the farthermost ends of the earth, depending on the situation. Recall our rule for enjoying life to the fullest extent, yet still retaining our cherished virtue of arising one day and walking away from it.

Be warned, even intelligent, highly successful people, often fail in living up to this divine virtue in life. Three who leap into mind are a well noted upstart actor, who is also a lower level country music performer. He married a once famous movie star, now turned high school music instructor, and is the respected owner of an amazingly successful physical and online herbal shop. Please don't ask me for the names, however, since I am certain readers already know, if only one dares search out the deepest recesses of his or her mind.

A highly successful real estate investor, who published best selling how-to books, hosts televised events in regard to real-estate investing, is very visible and active; failed terribly in living up to our fore-stated golden virtue. Please don't be so rude as to request names or specifics in regard to these vague descriptions given for these otherwise interesting people! I am only attempting to make a point here in their mentioning.

While these good folks, and no doubt numerous others not mentioned, all eventually over came the deluge of adversity attached to their published need for servicing a multiplicity of vices, as it may; sadly yet realistically,  fortune born from adversity due to such concerns, may not turn so easily for us. For those of us who must thrive down here on the Kansas farm, our golden life rule is always paramount.


(4) My final direct marketing technique is to *rent a display table at book shows and literary festivals held across America.* More than likely books shows and literary festivals will be held in places encouraging growth of a literary community, and devoted to promoting literacy in general. Towns dedicated to promoting the arts and the artistic, festival community, will be places where our cherished events are held.

In other words, if one has been following the advice in this pamphlet/mini-book, he has already long since donated his work to libraries and Little Free Libraries in the area. There may be a chance he has already courted a small following inside these localities. Intellectual types and people who love to read in general, especially children, love to visit books shows and literary festivals. Publishing reps, agents, editors, and reps from book distributors also love to visit.

In short, renting a table at these events is virtually *never a bad idea* for writers and established authors to do. Often the rental fees are not bad, only 20 to 100 dollars, American, maybe. Sometimes one may secure a place for free, but not often.

One time I was so poor I couldn't afford to purchase but twelve copies of my own work to display and sell. I sold every copy at full price. I also distributed hundreds of my blog cards. I told curious people about my work, and passed out homemade pamphlets going into great detail. I met and conversed with literary agents, editors, many fellow writers, and one local news reporter. This particular literary event was held on a huge plantation estate near an interesting town called Monk's Corner. Only visiting the grounds soaked heavily in tradition and history, being in literary company, and meeting all the interesting politicians, artists, and business people alike, made my day spent all worth while by far!

## Other thoughts and concerns

Finding employment in one's chosen field is maybe the greatest help for success in any specific field, on top of what has already been discussed. The situation of our present age in regard to the overall scenario and hiring process, in some ways makes doing so much more difficult than ever before for many, but especially for writers. Benefits aspiring authors can possibly find via writing as one's primary avenue of employment, however, and a possibility for developing direct publishing contacts, simply cannot be overstated.

Back in the days of Fitzgerald and Hemmingway, landing employment as a newspaper reporter, Hollywood script writer, or magazine reporter/writer, was simply a matter of one demonstrating where he stood in possession of a natural talent for success, in a majority of instances. At the time applicants were far less than the available opportunities.

Often I wonder had the editor at Scribners not given Fitzgerald a break on his first novel by recognizing his talent, had Hemmingway's family friend not landed him a staff writer job with the *Toranto Star Weekly* and later as an editor at the Chicago *Cooperative Commonwealth* , how might they have ended up ? Or better yet, had these same personalities came up in our own day of employing *entities at large disregarding natural talent and individual ambition for magisterial endorsed credentials and officially sanctioned hiring choices based on political agenda,* would these personalities have been the same literary success stories in our own time?  Might the fate of Edgar Allen Poe or H.P. Lovecraft have been that of the two famous names mentioned, and many more now famous authors, to include the one mentioned farther down on this page?

In our own day authors have taken the manuscripts of iconic literature such as *Pride & Prejudice,* changed the title and the first page, submitting it to more than 100 publishing editors at top houses, only to have it rejected every time, with rather disturbingly unerring consistency. How are writers supposed to interpret this phenomenon as it relates to writing and publishing opportunities in our own day?

My favorite story along above considerations, is one of a writer famous as Hemmingway in his own day, yet virtually forgotten in our time. His name is *Robert Ruark*, Ruark grew up on the edge of Wilmington, NC. Inside only ten years his old home place has become a historical site, if available information is understood correctly. Directly out of high-school Raurk lands employment as a reporter with a local newspaper in Southport, NC, a near impossible feat in our own time, in and of itself. Two years later his employment was terminated for being drunk on the job.

Ruark relocates farther inland to Sanford, NC. He lands employment as a reporter at a local newspaper there. There again, extraordinarily difficult to pull off in today's employment climate. Two years later he was terminated again for mysterious reasons, more than likely on-site drunkenness . This would make him 20 -22 years old at the time, with a horrible employment record by today's standards.

With two back to back terminations for being drunk on the job, imagine one's self today seeking employment as an upstart writer today for a moment!

Raurk relocates to Washington, D.C., where he secures employment as a reporter again, but this time at one of America's most prestigious newspapers, *The Washington Tribune;* following two employment terminations, more than likely due to drunkenness on the job. In our own day landing employment at the Washington Tribune would be an *extraordinary feat,* even with a perfect employment record, not to mention a writing portfolio to accompany a myriad stack of degrees, various certifications, complete with personal and professional endorsements systemically validating some previously deduced station of experience established for a basic entry level consideration alone as a writer.

Raurk remained there twenty years, became a foreign correspondent, and eventually a very famous writer; following in near exact footsteps of Hemmingway, as far as this author is concerned. Such would constitute the one note of Raurk's life this author doesn't admire. Why couldn't he design his own lifestyle to live by? His writing is extraordinary, nevertheless. Rather than death by suicide, as Hemmingway did at age 63, Raurk perished from excessive alcohol consumption at age 50, two years after the death of Hemmingway. I ask the question again here in this paragraph's last sentence; *what would good ole Robert Raurk have done, had he came up in our present age?* Might Raurk have ever amounted to anything other than only being a frustrated, embittered drunk, much less an employed writer, let alone a famous literary personality in his own day?

While its nice to aspire and make an effort, these employment options may or may not be available to us aspiring authors in our own time. Thankfully we have other options. The internet is filled with an assortment of paying opportunities for writers. *Odesk* is a good place to seek our work, as is *Freelance gigs.com . Craig's list* is another great place to search. There is also *Smart Blogger, Flex Jobs,*

*Contena, and Bonsai.* I have a second cousin who works for an insurance company writing claims reports, and a first cousin who teaches creative writing at Western Carolina University.

I, myself, frequently do research projects, take online college courses for clients, write research papers, and have ghost written on a number of occasions, simply because it pays decently. Unless *authors can slyly craft veiled notes into the ghost written scrip,* directing readers back to his or her *author's landing pad (blog with links to one's work, author page, etc),* as I call it, there is no long term advantage in ghost writing, or doing any of the above underneath the name of a paying client. In ways being a ghost writer, doing research papers for clients, or taking online college courses for customers; is strikingly reminiscent of participation in the adult entertainment industry, or outright prostitution. We, authors, craft every move exactly to the whim of our paying clientele, then we spend ourselves up as we pleasure them, with absolutely nothing being present giving us fulfillment in the long term.

While teaching school requires a systemically endorsed degree and state certification, working at a publishing company or in some small local periodical at a bottom level, may not. In any case here, the general idea is to develop direct publishing contacts online or in person, and become employed in a scenario where one utilizes his writing talent on a daily basis. Sometimes I find myself believing having contacts is better than skill, education, or work ethic; although we always want to carry all of these positives to our table, especially with personal records being kept so closely and with such great detail in our own day.

## Conclusion

I certainly hope every reader and listener has gained some bit of useful information from this work. Writing it caused me to revisit some dearly departed memories, while recalling a few very interesting experiences, especially during the early weeks and months of the Covid 19 era. It was fun riding around to visit the libraries, drop boxes, and LFLs in my own town and surrounding areas. During the C-19 era, riding around, writing, and making submissions kept me very busy, when I would have been extraordinarily bored to the extent of pulling my hair out otherwise.

I've certainly had fun in my great adventure as a tradesman, traveling adventurer, an author, teacher, lecturer, and being a creative person in general, as I sincerely hope you will. Maybe next time I will have that best seller with the huge contract and the fifty thousand dollar advance, eh? When I do, all of my dear readers and information seekers shall indeed be the first to know! More importantly, all of them will also possess the knowledge to replicate my own personal success, with an extraordinary exactness. So with that, until next time....

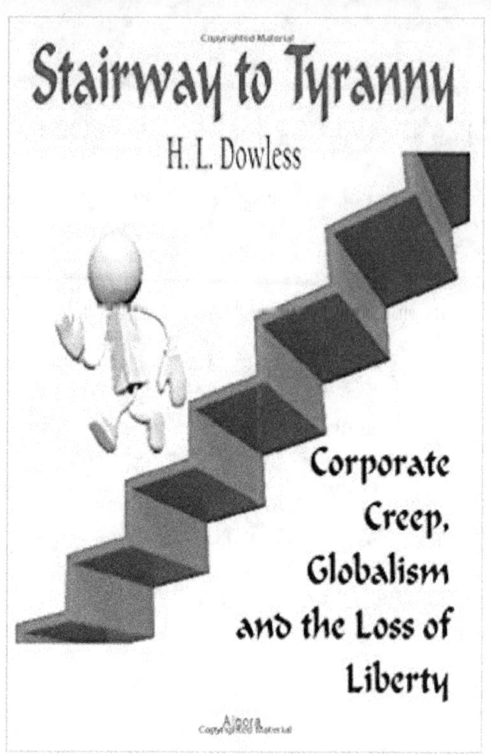

Stairway to Tyranny
H. L. Dowless
Corporate
Creep,
Globalism
and the Loss of
Liberty
Algora

Reflections on the
Loss of the Freeborn
American Nation
H. L. Dowless

MARCH OF THE
DIVINE
MAGNIFICENT
H. L. DOWLESS

Another
Lifetime
ccid

JustFiction!
Edition
Once Upon A Time In Nottoway
A tale of the wanton, the fantastic and the sincere
H.L. Dowless

JustFiction!
Edition
The Old Dirt Road And
The Hellion
A living breathing portrait of art
Lynn Dowless

JustFiction!
Edition
Thea Stelanofotos
from Nymphania on the hill
H.L. Dowless